Sally Gets a Job

Written and Illustrated by
Stephen Huneck

Abrams Books for Young Readers
New York

ARTIST'S NOTE

I have hand-carved wood blocks to make prints
for a number of years. For the first time, I'm
experimenting with using color pencils atop the
woodcuts to give the artwork additional feeling.
It is subtle, but as my thoughts about my artwork
evolve, so do the mediums I choose to use. Each
artwork is a hand-carved woodblock print with
color pencil on paper.

Library of Congress Cataloging-in-Publication Data:
Huneck, Stephen.
Sally gets a job / by Stephen Huneck.
p. cm.
Summary: While her family is away at work and school, Sally, a
black labrador retriever, dreams of all the jobs she might get, then
remembers that she already has the best job of all.
ISBN-13: 978-0-8109-9493-5 [hardcover w/jkt.]
[1. Labrador retriever—Fiction. 2. Dogs—Fiction.
3. Occupations—Fiction.] I. Title.
PZ7.H8995Saj 2008
[E]—dc22
2007012757

Text and illustrations copyright © 2008 Stephen Huneck
Book design by Vivian Cheng

Printed and bound in China
10 9 8 7 6 5 4 3 2 1

HNA
harry n. abrams, inc.
a subsidiary of La Martinière Groupe

115 West 18th Street
New York, NY 10011
www.hnabooks.com

It's a lucky dog that has a family,
and it's a lucky family that has a dog.

There they go, off to work and school.
I wish I could go, too.
Maybe I should get a job.

I would love to be the school bus driver.

Better yet, I could be a teacher.

A zoo might be a great place to work.

I could feed the elephants.

But cleaning up afterward
may be harder than I think.

Some dogs make great guards,
but I don't think it is for me.

Though being a
lifeguard sounds like fun.

I like to dig in the sand.

Maybe I could be an archaeologist.

Or maybe I should just focus on bones
and become a paleontologist.

I also love playing ball.
Maybe I could turn pro.

I like people, and people like me.
Maybe I should run for president.

Though I have never seen one, I think it would be fun to be a hip-hop star.

Studying nature is a lot of fun.
Nothing about it bugs me.

Every time I visit the pond, I get frogs on the brain. Maybe I should be a biologist.

I could become a rescue dog
and rescue cats from trees.

Every time I visit the pond, I get frogs on the brain. Maybe I should be a biologist.

I could become a rescue dog
and rescue cats from trees.

Or even burning buildings.
What a hero I would be!

Farming might be good.
I would get to drive a tractor . . .

and making maple syrup in the
early spring would be really yummy.

I could become a chef and
open a fine restaurant.

It would be a lot of work cooking and cleaning,
but washing the dishes would be tasty.

I am very psychic. I can always tell when my family is about to arrive.

I am so happy they are home.
I realize now I have the best job in the world:

Taking care of my family.